This Book Belongs to:

Friendship Saves the Day

By Karen Ravn

Illustrated by Cary Phillips

Miss Penelope Pig said in her weekly advice column in the local newspaper, "The time has come for everyone to do some spring cleaning." So Lainie Lamb got up at dawn to start hers.

Now to be perfectly honest, Lainie's house was small, and nothing in it was very dirty in the first place. By 10 o'clock, she had dusted and mopped and scrubbed and waxed and polished just about everything in sight. In fact, the only things left to wash were the curtains.

Lainie had saved the curtains for last because she liked them so much. And she liked them so much because she was so proud of them. And she was so proud of them because she had made them herself!

Very, very carefully, Lainie took the curtains down and washed them in the sink and then spread them outside on the lilac bushes to dry. All the while, she kept noticing how beautiful they were. "If I do say so myself," she said, "these are probably the most beautiful curtains in the world!"

When her cleaning was done, Lainie Lamb decided to celebrate by visiting her good friend Gallagher Goat, who lived just down the road. When she got to Gallagher's house, there was a sign on the door that said "Gone for lunch."

Lainie considered waiting for Gallagher to come back, but she knew that sometimes he took very long lunches. Gallagher REALLY liked to eat!

So Lainie turned around and went home again, and guess what was gone when she got there—

"My curtains!" Lainie Lamb cried. "My beautiful curtains! Where could they be?" One thing was clear. They weren't drying in the sun on the lilac bushes where she had left them.

Then Lainie heard a sleepy voice from under the apple tree. "What's all this commotion?" the voice said. "Can't a gentleman get any rest around here?"

"Oh, Sir Sheldon Snail," Lainie said, for the sleepy voice belonged to that noble snail, who was just now poking his head out of his shell. "I didn't even see you there!" said Lainie. "But tell me, where do you think my curtains could be?"

"Your curtains?" Sir Sheldon Snail asked. "Don't you think they might be inside your house, hanging in front of your windows?"

"No, no," Lainie said. And then she explained why not.

"Well, I haven't seen a thing," Sir Sheldon Snail said. "But then, I'm off to sort of a slow start this morning."

Lainie didn't mention that it was already afternoon or that Sir Sheldon Snail got off to a slow start every day. She liked him too much to hurt his feelings, and besides, she was too worried about her curtains.

"Maybe the wind blew my curtains away," Lainie Lamb said, "except there isn't any wind today."

"What didn't the wind blow away?" asked two cheery voices both at once. There at Lainie's gate stood Lonnie and Bonnie Bunny, who always said and did everything together.

"My curtains!" Lainie said. And then she told her whole story again.

"What a shame!" said Lonnie and Bonnie. "We're going to the store, and we'll keep our eyes open."

"The store?" asked Sir Sheldon, who had noticed that Lonnie and Bonnie had their little red wagon with them. "I wish I could go to the store,

but it's so very far from here. Won't it take days and days to get there?"

"Not for us!" Lonnie and Bonnie said together. "Would you like a ride?"

"Why, what a nice idea," Sir Sheldon said. "I never would have thought of that. I suppose that wagon of yours is just the right size for a gentleman like me."

"Of course, Sir Sheldon," Lonnie and Bonnie said. "You're our friend, so we're happy to give you a ride."

Lonnie and Bonnie Bunny lifted Sir Sheldon Snail into their wagon and set off down the road.

No sooner were they gone than Lulu Ladybug dropped by with her son, Little Louie. Lainie Lamb told her story again. She was getting very good at it.

"I remember your curtains," Lulu said. "And you're right. They were very beautiful."

"Yes, veeerrry boo-tee-ful!" exclaimed Little Louie.

"Come along, Little Louie," Lulu said. "Let's go fly around a little and see if we can find those curtains for Lainie." And off they went.

Two seconds later, Gallagher Goat trotted up. "I've just been for a walk after lunch," he said. "And a very yummy lunch it was, too! Why, it was one of the yummiest lunches I ever tasted."

Lainie didn't ask Gallagher what yummy stuff he had eaten for lunch, because she didn't want to know. Lainie thought Gallagher liked to eat very strange things.

Instead, Lainie told him the curtain story she was so good at telling.

"Hmmmmm," Gallagher said. "And these curtains of yours, what do they look like?"

"They have pink and white stripes," Lainie said. "And lace ruffles. And they're very clean—and very beautiful!"

"Oh my!" Gallagher said as a sad look came over his face. "Oh my! Oh my! Oh my!"

"What's wrong?" Lainie asked.

"I'm afraid," Gallagher said, "that your curtains very much resemble my lunch."

"You ate my curtains!" Lainie cried. "How could you, Gallagher? Nobody eats curtains! Everybody knows that!"

"Oh, dear! I think I'm in trouble now! I'm sorry, Lainie!" he blurted out as he quickly ran away.

Lainie sat down on the porch and thought about how beautiful her poor curtains had been and how mad she was at Gallagher for eating them. "That goat!" she said. "He's always eating things he shouldn't! But I guess I told him!" Then, as she thought about how mad she had been at Gallagher, she felt terrible.

At that very moment, Miss Penelope Pig came by. Miss Penelope wrote an advice column in the paper, and Lainie surely needed some advice right now! "Dear Miss Penelope," Lainie said, "I have this friend who ate up my beautiful curtains that I made my very own self. So I got really mad at him, and he ran off to hide. What would you say about that?"

"I'd say your friend must be awfully hungry," said Miss Penelope, who considered herself as witty as she was wise. "I'd also say your friend must be Gallagher Goat. Whatever are we going to do about him?"

She sat down next to Lainie, and together they planned exactly what to do about Gallagher.

A little while later, Lainie set off on a walk. First she went to Granville Groundhog's house. Granville, the weather forecaster, was standing by his front gate looking up at the blue sky. "I don't like to brag," he said, "but the weather is very nice today, isn't it?" Granville liked to take credit for the weather when it was good, although he didn't much like to take any blame for it when it was bad.

"Yes," Lainie said, "it's very nice. But tell me, is it still going to be nice later this afternoon?"

Granville took a big bunch of notes out of his vest pocket and studied them for a while. "I predict 100 percent chance of sun," he said finally, "unless we get some showers, in which case I predict 100 percent chance of rain."

"That makes sense," Lainie said. "But I do hope it's sunny." And then she told him the secret about Gallagher Goat.

When she left Granville, Lainie headed for Brad Badger's house because she knew it was Garden Club day. Pretty soon she heard footsteps behind her and a tiny little voice calling her name. It was Mitzi Mouse.

"I'm in charge of refreshments today," Mitzi squeaked. "So I brought cheesecake. I just love cheesecake. Don't you just love cheesecake?"

Just then, from out of the blue, a green blur came whizzing past them. "Hi! Bye!" said the blur.

"That must have been Fritz Frog," said Lainie.

"He's such a quiet frog," said Mitzi. "He's so shy he never stops to talk."

But when they got to Brad's house, Fritz Frog had stopped to rest.

"Are you coming to the meeting?" Mitzi asked him. "I didn't know you were a gardener."

"Oh, yes!" said Fritz Frog. "I'm learning how to garden from Brad Badger. I do have quite a green thumb. In fact, I have two!" And he held up both his green hands.

TODAY'S SPEAKER
MYRA MOLE

Brad Badger was setting up chairs on the lawn, and Priscilla Opossum was already sitting in one of them. "Please sit here next to me," Priscilla said to Lainie, "and make sure I don't fall asleep during Myra's speech. She'd never forgive me." Lainie noticed that Priscilla had brought along her pillow, just in case.

"I'm sorry," Lainie said. "I can't stay. I'm just here to talk to Brad."

The front of Brad's vest was covered with ribbons and badges. "Did you win all of those for your gardening?" Lainie asked. She always asked Brad that question because she knew how much he liked to answer it.

"Yes, indeed," he said. "I have 43 of them altogether, I do believe."

"That's amazing," Lainie said. Then she told him what she had come to say, and Brad promised to make an announcement about Gallagher at the meeting.

Lainie continued on to the swimming pond. Trevor Turtle was sitting under an umbrella, planning his next trip, which would also be his first. And Piper Pony and Benson Bear were having a picnic. "Want to join us?" Piper asked. "There's plenty of hay!"

"And plenty of honey!" Benson Bear added.

But Lainie especially wanted to see Dipsy Duck. She had expected to find her swimming, but she wasn't. She was just sitting on the bank looking sad. "Is something wrong?" Lainie asked. "Has anything happened?"

"No, nothing's happened," Dipsy said. "That's just the problem. I haven't heard any interesting gossip—I mean, news—since I can't remember when."

Then Lainie told her about Gallagher Goat, and right away Dipsy cheered up. "Wow!" she said. "I'll pass the word along. You can count on me."

Lainie Lamb returned home and tried very hard not to look at her bare windows. Then she went outside and picked a bouquet of flowers before setting off down the road toward Gallagher's house again.

She stopped behind a grove of trees where Gallagher couldn't see her. This was where everyone was supposed to meet. And sure enough, pretty soon, along came Miss Penelope. She had a bunch of old newspapers with her. "All my old columns," she said. "I don't need them anymore."

Then Priscilla Opossum showed up with an extra pillow. "This one's no good," she said. "It's all smooshed."

Then Brad Badger came with a sack full of weeds. And Dipsy Duck came with some tin cans she'd found at the bottom of the pond. And Granville Groundhog came with a broken-down weather vane.

And then Benson Bear came with some almost empty jars of honey. And Piper Pony came with a fuzzy old blanket.

And then Myra Mole came with some crumbly mud pies. And Mitzi Mouse came with a saggy cheese souffle.

Before long, just about everybody was there, and they had all brought along something old or stale or broken or just plain yucky.

Everyone else stayed behind in the trees while Lainie Lamb went to knock on Gallagher's door. When he answered, he still looked sad. "I'm sorry I was so rude," Lainie said. "I feel pretty sheepish."

"I don't blame you, though," Gallagher Goat said. "It was terrible of me to eat your beautiful curtains."

"They were beautiful," Lainie said. "They were truly beautiful curtains. But never mind, because I can always make new curtains, but I could never make a new friend like you."

"Speaking of new curtains..." Gallagher said. Before he could finish, Lainie handed him the flowers that she'd picked.

"Here," she said. "These are for you."

"Golly," Gallagher said. "Thank you, Lainie."

"You can eat them if you want," Lainie said.

"Oh, no!" Gallagher Goat said. "I'm turning over a new leaf. From now on, I'm going to be much more careful about what I eat."

"Okay," Lainie Lamb said. "But please don't start yet. Please don't start until after the party!"

And suddenly the whole crowd of Gallagher's friends came up the walk with all their goodies.

"Oh my, oh my, oh my, oh my!" Gallagher said. "You shouldn't have done this! And look! You brought all my favorite junk food!"

"We found this junk—I mean, junk food—doing our spring cleaning—just as I'd suggested in my column," said Miss Penelope Pig. "We wanted to surprise you."

"I have a surprise for you, too," Gallagher Goat said. And then he called into his house—"Lulu! Little Louie!"

Out came the two ladybugs, mother and son, carrying lots and lots and lots and lots of yellow and white polka-dot material.

"For new curtains!" Gallagher said. "It was Lulu's idea."

"Actually, it was Little Louie's idea to make Lainie Lamb some new curtains," said Lulu.

"If we all work together, we can have them done in no time!" said Gallagher.

And that is just exactly what they did.

"I used to love the old curtains that I'd made myself," Lainie said when they were all finished. "I thought they were the most beautiful curtains in the world. But now I LOVE my new curtains better—because the most wonderful friends in the world made them for me!"